Best Loved Stories

WIND IN THE WILLOWS

The River Bank

The Mole had been working hard all morning, spring cleaning his little underground home, first with brooms, then with dusters; then on ladders and chairs, with a brush and whitewash, till he had dust in his throat and eyes, splashes of whitewash all over his black fur, an aching back and weary arms.

Spring was moving in the air above, and in the earth below and around him. Small wonder, then, that he suddenly flung down his brush, said, "Bother!" and, "Oh, blow!" and also, "Hang spring cleaning!" and rushed out of the house.

He scraped and scratched and scrabbled and scrooged, then scrooged and scrabbled and scratched and scraped, working busily with his little paws, muttering, "Up we go! Up we go!" until at last, pop! his snout came out into the sunlight, and he found himself rolling in the warm grass of a meadow.

"This is fine!" he said. "This is better than white-washing!"

It all seemed too good to be true. He rambled through the meadow, where birds were building, flowers budding and leaves thrusting, till suddenly he came to a river. Never in his life had he seen a river before — and the Mole was fascinated.

As he sat on the bank and looked across the river, a dark hole on the opposite bank, just above the water's edge, caught his eye, and a small face appeared in it.

A little brown face, with whiskers; small neat ears and thick, silky hair. It was the Water Rat.

"Hello, Mole!" said the Water Rat.

"Hello, Rat!" said the Mole.

"Would you like to come over?" asked the Rat, who unfastened a rope and pulled on it, and stepped into a little boat, painted blue outside and white inside, and just the size for two animals.

The Rat sculled across, made fast, and helped the Mole into the boat. As the Rat shoved off the Mole sat down. "Do you know, I've never been in a boat before," he said.

"What?" cried the Rat. "Why, it's the only thing. There is nothing — absolutely nothing — so much worth doing as simply messing about in boats. In or out of 'em, it doesn't matter. Why don't we go down the river together, and make a day of it?"

The Rat went into his hole and reappeared with a fat wicker picnic basket. "What's inside?" asked Mole.

"There's cold chicken inside it," the Rat replied. " Coldtonguecoldhamcoldbeefpickledgherkinssalad frenchrollscresssandwichespottedmeatgingerbeer lemonadesodawater — "

"Stop!" cried the Mole happily. "This is too much!"

"Do you think so?" the Rat asked seriously. "It's only what I always take on these little trips."

The Mole didn't hear a word he was saying. He was lost in the sparkle, the ripple, the scents and the sounds of the river. He trailed a paw in the water and dreamed dreams while the Water Rat sculled steadily along.

After half an hour or so the Mole pulled himself together. "You must think me very rude," he said, "but all this is so new to me. So you live by the river?"

"By it and with it and on it and in it," said the Rat. "It's brother and sister to me, and food and drink and (naturally) washing. It's my world, and I don't want any other. In winter or summer, spring or autumn, it's got lots of fun and excitement."

Leaving the main stream, the Rat brought the boat alongside a grassy bank, and the Mole unpacked the picnic basket. "Now, pitch in, old fellow!" said the Rat, and the Mole was glad to do just that.

The two friends spent an enjoyable afternoon on the bank, and the sun was getting low as the Rat sculled gently homewards. Presently the Mole said, "Ratty! Please, I want to row now!"

The Rat shook his head with a smile. "Not yet," he said. "Wait till you've had a few lessons. It's not so easy as it looks."

But the Mole did not listen, and he suddenly jumped up and seized the sculls, knocking the Rat backwards off his seat. "Stop it!" cried the Rat. "You can't do it! You'll have us over!"

The Mole made a dig at the water, missed, and found himself lying on top of the Rat. Alarmed, he grabbed at the side of the boat, and — *sploosh!* — over went the boat.

How cold the water was, how it sang in his ears as he went down, down, down. Then a firm paw gripped him by the back of the neck, propelled him to the shore, and hauled him out, a squashy lump of misery.

When the Rat had rubbed him down a bit he said, "Now, trot up and down the towpath till you're warm and dry again, while I dive for the picnic basket."

When they set off for home again the Mole was limp and dejected. "Ratty, I am very sorry for my foolish conduct," he said. "I have been a complete ass, and I know it. Will you forgive me, and let things go on as before?"

"That's all right," said the Rat cheerily. "What's a little wet to a Water Rat? Look, I think you should come and stop with me for a time. I'll teach you to row and to swim, and you'll soon be as handy on the water as any of us."

When they got home the Rat made a fire in the parlour and planted the Mole in an armchair in front of it, having fetched him a dressing-gown and slippers, and told him river stories till supper time. Thrilling stories they were, too, about weirs, and sudden floods, and leaping pike; about herons, and adventures down drains, and night fishing with Otter, or excursions with Badger.

Soon after supper a very sleepy Mole had to be taken upstairs to the best bedroom, where he soon

laid his head on his pillow in great peace and contentment, knowing that his new-found friend, the River, was lapping at the window sill.

This day was the first of many similar ones for the Mole, each of them longer and more interesting as the summer moved on. He learnt to swim and to row, and entered into the joy of running water.

The Open Road

"Ratty," said the Mole suddenly one bright summer morning. "I want to ask you a favour. Will you take me to call on Mr Toad? I've heard so much about him, and I'd like to meet him."

"Certainly," said the Rat. "Get the boat out, and we'll paddle up there. It's never the wrong time to call on Toad. He's always good tempered, always glad to see you, always sorry when you go. Perhaps he's not very clever — we can't always be geniuses — and he may be boastful and conceited, but he has some great qualities, has Toady."

Later, rounding a bend in the river, they saw a handsome old house of red brick, with well-kept lawns reaching down to the water's edge.

"There's Toad Hall," said the Rat. "Toad is rather rich, you know."

They found Toad in a wicker chair, a large map spread out on his knees. "Hooray!" he cried. "This is splendid! Come with me!"

Toad led the way to the stable yard, where they

saw a gipsy caravan, shining with newness, painted a canary yellow picked out with green, with red wheels.

"There you are!" cried Toad. "There's real life for you, in that little cart. The open road, the dusty highway, the heath, the common, the hedgerows, the rolling downs! Camps, villages, towns, cities! Here today, and up and off to somewhere else to-morrow! The whole world before you!"

Inside there were bunks, a little folding table, a stove, lockers, bookshelves, a bird cage with a bird in it, and pots, pans, jugs and kettles of every size. "All complete," said the Toad, "biscuits, potted lobster, sardines, soda water, baccy, bacon, jam, cards, dominoes. You'll find nothing has been forgotten when we start this afternoon."

"Did I hear you say *we,* and *start,* and *this after-noon?*" said the Rat.

"You've *got* to come. You surely don't mean to stick to your dull old river all your life? I want to show you the *world*! Come and have some lunch," Toad said, "and we'll talk it over."

During luncheon Toad talked of the trip and the joys of the open road in such glowing colours that Mole could hardly sit in his chair he was so excited. It soon seemed that the trip was settled and the Rat allowed his good nature to take over. He could not bear to disappoint his two friends, and agreed to go with them.

An old grey horse was caught and harnessed and they set off, all talking at once.

It was a golden afternoon and it was late in the evening when, tired and happy and miles from home, they drew up on a common and ate their simple supper sitting on the grass, a yellow moon to keep them company.

Next day, they were strolling along the high road when, far behind, they heard a faint warning hum, like the drone of a distant bee. Glancing back, they saw a small cloud of dust advancing on them at incredible speed. In an instant the peaceful scene was changed, and with a blast of wind and a whirl of sound, it was on them! They had a moment's glimpse of glittering plate glass and rich leather, and the magnificent motor car was gone.

The old grey horse reared, plunged — and drove the cart backwards. There was a crash — and the canary-coloured cart lay on its side in the deep ditch at the side of the road, a complete wreck.

The Rat and the Mole tried to right the cart, but could not, and they tried to enlist Toad's help.

They found him in a sort of trance, a happy smile on his face. "Glorious, stirring sight!" he murmured. "The poetry of motion! The *real* way to travel! The *only* way to travel! I've done with carts for ever!"

The Rat and the Mole took a still day-dreaming Toad home by train, and sculled down the river to Rat's home.

The next evening the Rat had news for the Mole. "Heard the news?" he said. "Toad went to town this morning and ordered a large and very expensive motor car."

The Wild Wood

One winter afternoon, when the Rat was dozing in front of the fire in his armchair, the Mole decided to explore the Wild Wood, and perhaps meet Mr Badger, for he had heard such a lot about him.

There was nothing to alarm him at first. Twigs crackled under his feet, logs tripped him, and he went in deeper, where the light was less.

Then the faces began.

It was over his shoulder that he first thought he saw a face, but when he turned it had gone.

He hurried on, telling himself not to imagine things, but suddenly there were faces everywhere.

Then the whistling began.

Very faint and shrill it was, far behind him, and it made him hurry forward. Then, still very faint and shrill, it sounded far ahead of him, and made him want to go back.

Then the pattering began.

It was the pat-pat-pat of little feet, and seemed to be closing in on him. The whole world seemed to be running, hunting, chasing, closing in on something — or somebody? In panic, the Mole began to run, too. He ran against things, fell over things and into things, darted under things and dodged round things.

At last he took refuge in the dark deep hollow of an old beech tree, snuggling down into the dry leaves there, hoping he was safe. As he lay there, panting and trembling, he knew the awful thing other animals had whispered of — the Terror of the Wild Wood!

Meantime, the Rat had woken, found Mole missing — and had followed his tracks into the Wild Wood, looking anxiously on either side for any sign of his friend. "Moly, Moly!" he called. "Where are you? It's me — it's old Rat!"

He had hunted through the wood for an hour or more when from the hole in the beech tree came a feeble voice. "Ratty! Is that really you?" it said.

The Rat crept into the hollow. "You really

shouldn't have come here on your own, Mole," he said. "We river-bankers hardly ever come here by ourselves. We'll make a start for home soon, when you've had a rest."

But when they left the hole, they found that snow had fallen. "Well, it can't be helped," said the Rat. "The worst of it is, I don't exactly know where we are."

An hour or two later they stopped, weary and hopeless. They were aching and bruised, and the snow was getting so deep that they could hardly drag their little legs through it. There seemed to be no end to the wood, and no way out.

"We can't sit here for long," said the Rat. "We'll try and find shelter, a cave or hole out of the snow and wind, and we'll have a good rest before we try again."

They struggled down into a dell, and suddenly the Mole tripped up and fell forward with a squeal.

The Rat saw what Mole had fallen over — and started to cry, "Hooray!" Then he scraped in the snow and uncovered a door mat. "Scrape and scratch and dig and hunt around!" the Rat told Mole. "It's our only chance!"

Mole soon saw what the Rat was so excited about. In the side of what had seemed to be a snow-bank was a little door, painted dark green. On a small brass plate they read: MR BADGER.

The Mole fell backwards on the snow from sheer surprise. "Rat!" he cried. "You're a wonder!"

Mr Badger

"Badger," cried the Rat. "Let us in, please. It's me, Rat, and my friend Mole, and we've lost our way in the snow."

"Ratty, my dear little man!" exclaimed the Badger. "Come along in, both of you."

The Badger led them down a long, gloomy passage into a central hall. Badger flung open a door, and they found themselves in the glow and warmth of a large fire-lit kitchen.

The kindly Badger sat them to toast themselves by the fire, fetched dressing-gowns and slippers, and bathed Mole's shin. Warm and dry at last, the Mole and the Rat ate the supper that Badger had prepared for them, then Badger said, "Now then! How's old Toad?"

"Oh, from bad to worse," said the Rat. "Another smash-up only last week."

"How many has he had?" inquired the Badger.

"Smashes or motor cars?" asked the Rat. "Oh, well, it's the same thing with Toad. This is the seventh."

"And he's been in hospital three times," put in the Mole.

"We're his friends," Rat said. "Shouldn't we do something?"

"Yes," said Badger. "Once the year has turned, and the nights are shorter, we'll take Toad in hand. We'll *make* him be a sensible Toad!"

Ratty and Mole slept at Badger's that night, and in the morning they had a visitor — the Otter. "I thought I'd find you here," he said. "They were in a state along River Bank, talking of something dreadful happening to you. But I knew that when people were in a fix they mostly went to Badger, so I came straight here."

After lunch, Badger took the Mole on a tour of his home while Otter and Rat talked river-talk, and when they got back the Rat was anxious to leave for home. Badger led the way along a long tunnel, said a hasty goodbye, and pushed them through the opening.

They found themselves on the very edge of the Wild Wood, and turned for home.

Dulce Domum (Home Sweet Home)

One winter evening the Mole and the Water Rat were returning home after a long day's outing with Otter. They were in high spirits, with much chatter and laughter.

"It looks as if we're coming to a village," said the Mole as they came to a road.

"Oh, never mind!" said the Rat. "At this season of the year they're all safe indoors by this time, sitting round the fire: men, women, children, dogs and cats and all. We can have a look at them through their windows, if you like, and see what they're doing."

As they approached the village there was a first thin fall of powdery snow. Little was visible but squares of dusky orange-red on either side of the street, where the firelight or lamplight of each cottage overflowed through the windows into the dark world outside.

The Mole and the Rat moved from one home to another and, so far from home themselves, watched wistfully as a cat was stroked, a sleepy child picked up and huddled off to bed, or a tired man stretched and knocked out his pipe on the end of a smouldering log.

Then a gust of bitter wind, a small sting of frozen sleet woke them from their dream, and they knew their toes to be cold and their legs tired, and their own home a weary distance away.

Once beyond the village they could smell through the darkness the friendly fields again, and they braced themselves for the last long stretch, the home stretch, the stretch that we know is bound to end, some time, in the rattle of the door latch, the sudden firelight, and the sight of familiar things.

Suddenly Mole stopped dead in his tracks, his nose searching hither and thither, trying to capture the smell that had suddenly reached him, and had made him tingle.

Home! That was what it was, his old home that he had left behind, that day when he had first found the river! He had hardly given it a thought, and now it was telling him, through his nose, that it had missed him, and wanted him back.

"Ratty!" he called. "Come back! Please stop! You don't understand! It's my home, my old home! I've just come across the smell of it, and it's close. I must go to it! Please, please come back!"

Rat was too far ahead to hear clearly what the Mole was saying, and he hurried on. "We mustn't stop now!" he called back. "It's late, and the snow's coming on again, and I'm not sure of the way! Come on, quick, there's a good fellow!"

With a wrench that tore his very heart-strings, the Mole set off down the road after the Rat, and soon caught up with him.

When they sat down to rest, the Mole could control himself no longer and he sobbed and cried freely and helplessly.

The Rat was astonished. "What is it, old fellow?" he asked. "Whatever can be the matter?"

Poor Mole found it difficult to get the words out between sobs. "I know it's a — shabby little place," he sobbed, "not like — your cosy quarters — or Toad's beautiful hall — but it was my own little home — and I went away and forgot all about it — and then I smelt it suddenly — and you wouldn't turn back, Ratty — you wouldn't turn back!"

The Rat waited until Mole's sobs had quietened, then he set off again, back the way they had come. "We're going to find that home of yours," he said. "So cheer up, old chap, and take my arm, and we'll very soon be there."

They walked back along the road until Mole stood rigid, and his upturned nose, quivering slightly, sniffed the air. The Rat followed as the Mole crossed a dry ditch, scrambled through a hedge, nosed his way over a field, then suddenly, without warning, dived down a tunnel.

It was close and airless, and the earthy smell was strong, and it seemed a long time to Rat till he could stand erect. Then Mole struck a match, and the Rat saw that they were standing in an open space, neatly swept and sanded underfoot, and directly facing them was Mole's little front door, with 'Mole End' painted over the bell-pull at the side.

Mole took down a lantern from a nail on the wall and lit it, and the Rat saw that they were in a sort of forecourt. A garden seat stood on one side of the door, and on the walls hung wire baskets with ferns in them. Down one side ran a skittle alley, with benches along it and little wooden tables. In the middle was a small round pond with goldfish in it, surrounded by a cockleshell border.

Mole's face beamed at the sight of the objects so dear to him, and he hurried Rat through the door, lit a lamp in the hall, and looked at his old home. The dust lay thick on everything, and the house looked cheerless, deserted and neglected. "Oh, Ratty!" he cried. "Why did I do it? Why did I bring you to this poor, cold little place when you could have been at River Bank, toasting your toes in front of the fire?"

The Rat took no notice. He was running here and there, opening doors, inspecting rooms and cupboards, and lighting lamps and candles. "What a fine little house this is!" he called. "So compact! So well planned! We'll make a jolly night of it. The first thing we want is a good fire. I'll see to that, while you get a duster and smarten things up a bit."

Encouraged, the Mole dusted and polished with energy, while the Rat soon had a cheerful blaze roaring up the chimney.

Then Mole had another fit of the blues, and buried his face in his duster. "What about your supper?" he moaned. "I've nothing to give you — nothing — not a crumb!"

"What a fellow you are for giving in!" said the Rat. "Why, I saw a sardine-can opener in the kitchen,

and everybody knows that means there are sardines about. Come with me and look."

They hunted through every cupboard and turned out every drawer, and found a tin of sardines, a box of biscuits, nearly full — and a German sausage in silver paper.

"There's a banquet for you," said the Rat as he laid the table. "Now, what's that little door at the end of the passage? Your cellar, of course!"

He made for the cellar door, and soon emerged, dusty, with a bottle of beer in each paw and another under each arm. "This is really the jolliest little place I ever was in. Tell me all about it."

So, while Rat fetched plates, knives and forks, and mixed some mustard, the Mole told how this was planned, and how that was thought out, the Rat saying, "Wonderful," and, "Most remarkable," at intervals.

At last they sat down at the table, and the Rat had got to work with the sardine-can opener, when they heard sounds from the forecourt, sounds like the scuffling of small feet, and the murmur of tiny voices. Broken sentences reached them — "Now, all in a line — hold the lantern up a bit, Tommy — clear your throats first — no coughing after I say one, two, three."

"What's up?" asked the Rat.

"I think it must be the field mice," replied the Mole. "They go round carol singing at this time of year. They come to Mole End last of all, and I used to give them hot drinks, and supper too, when I could afford it. It will be like old times to hear them again."

"Let's have a look at them!" cried the Rat, and ran to the door.

It was a pretty sight that met their eyes. Lit by the dim rays of a lantern, eight or ten little field mice stood in a semi-circle, red scarves around their necks, their paws thrust deep into their pockets, their feet jigging for warmth. One of the elder ones said, "Now then, one, two, three!" and their shrill little voices rose into the air, singing one of the old-time carols.

"Very well sung, boys!" cried the Rat when they had finished. "And now come along in, all of you, and warm yourselves by the fire, and have something hot!"

"Yes, come along, field mice," cried the Mole. "This is quite like old times. Now, wait a minute while we — oh, Ratty!" he cried. "We've nothing to give them!"

"You leave that to me," said the Rat, calling the field mouse with the lantern. "Are your shops open at this hour?"

When he heard that they were, the Rat gave his order, and the Mole only heard bits of it, such as — "Fresh, mind! — see you get Buggin's — yes, of course, home made, no tinned stuff!" Finally, there was a chink of coin passing from paw to paw, and the field mouse hurried off.

The rest of the field mice perched on a wooden settle by the fire, and toasted their toes till they tingled. They even drank a little warmed beer, and soon forgot they had ever been cold.

Soon the field mouse with the lantern reappeared, staggering under the weight of his basket, and in a few minutes supper was ready. As they ate they talked of old times, and the field mice answered the hundred questions the Mole had to ask them.

They clattered off at last, and when the door had closed on the last of them, Mole and Rat kicked the fire up, drew their chairs in, brewed themselves a last nightcap, and discussed the events of the long day. At last the Rat, with a tremendous yawn, said, "Mole, old chap, I'm ready to drop. That your little sleeping bunk? Very well, then, I'll take this one. What a ripping little house this is! Everything so handy!"

He clambered into his bunk and rolled himself up

in the blankets, and soon Mole's head was on his pillow, too. But before he closed his eyes he let them wander round his old room, and saw clearly how much it all meant to him. He did not want to abandon his new life in the sun and air by the river, but it was good to think he had this to come back to, this place which was all his own.

Mr Toad

It was a bright morning in the early part of summer, and the Rat and the Mole were just finishing breakfast when there was a knock at the door.

"It's Mr Badger!" said Mole, letting him in.

"The hour has come!" said the Badger.

"What hour?" asked the Rat uneasily.

"Toad's hour," the Badger replied. "I said I would take him in hand after the winter. Another new and powerful motor car will arrive at Toad Hall this morning. We must go to the rescue."

Outside Toad Hall stood a shiny new red car and as they drew nearer Mr Toad came down the steps, in goggles, cap, gloves and overcoat.

"Take him inside," the Badger said sternly, "and take those silly clothes off him!"

"You knew it would come to this, Toad," the Badger said. "You're getting us animals a bad name with your furious driving and your smashes and your rows with the police. Come with me into the smoking room and hear some facts about yourself."

After some three quarters of an hour the Badger reappeared with a very limp and dejected Toad. His skin hung baggily, his legs wobbled, and his cheeks were streaked with tears.

Badger made Toad sit down. "I want you to repeat what you told me just now," said Badger. "That you're sorry for what you've done, and see the folly of it all."

There was a long, long pause, then Toad spoke. "No, I'm *not* sorry. And it wasn't folly at all! It was glorious!"

"What?" cried the Badger. "You don't promise never to touch a motor car again?"

"On the contrary," said Toad. "I promise that the first car I see, off I go in it!"

"Very well," said Badger. "You've often asked us to come and stay with you; now we're going to. Take him upstairs and lock him in!"

And Toad, kicking and struggling, was hauled upstairs by his two friends. . . .

Each animal took it in turn to sleep in Toad's room at night, and they divided the day up between them.

One fine morning the Rat went upstairs to relieve Badger, who was going for a run with Mole. He found Toad in a very feeble mood. "I'm a nuisance, I know," said Toad, "but could I beg you — for the last time, probably — to step round to the village — even now it may be too late — and fetch the doctor? And would you mind asking the lawyer to come too?"

The Rat was worried and, after locking the door behind him, set off for the village.

As soon as he had gone the Toad got dressed, knotted sheets together to make a rope, dropped to the ground, and marched off, whistling a merry tune.

When Badger and Mole returned Rat had to face them with his pitiful story. "He did it really well," said Rat, crestfallen.

"He did *you* well!" said the Badger.

Meanwhile, Toad was lunching at the Red Lion Inn. Coming outside, he found a car in the middle of the yard. "I wonder," he said to himself, "if this sort of car *starts* easily?"

Next moment, he was holding the starting handle

and turning it and, as if in a dream, found himself in the driver's seat. He swung the car round the yard and out, into open country. He was Toad once more, Toad the traffic-queller, before whom all must give way, reckless of what might happen.

"To my mind," said the Chairman of the Magistrates, "the only difficulty in this case is the length of sentence. He has been found guilty of stealing a car, of dangerous driving, and of gross impertience to the police. Mr Clerk?"

"You had better make it a round twenty years," said the Clerk of the Court.

And that is how Toad found himself a helpless prisoner in the remotest dungeon of the best-guarded, stoutest castle in all the length and breadth of Merry England.

Toad's Adventures

When Toad found himself in the dank dungeon he flung himself on the floor and shed bitter tears. "This is the end of everything," he said. "The end of the career of Toad, the popular and handsome Toad, the rich and hospitable Toad. Stupid animal that I was! Wise old Badger! Clever Rat and sensible Mole! They were right!"

He passed his days and nights like this for several weeks, refusing meals, until the gaoler's daughter took pity on him.

She coaxed him to eat, and he told her all about his life at Toad Hall. She thought it was a shame that Toad should be locked up for what seemed to her a very trivial offence, and decided to help him escape.

"Toad," she said one day, "please listen. I have an aunt who is a washerwoman."

"Never mind," said Toad kindly. "Think no more about it. *I* have several aunts who *ought* to be washerwomen."

"Do be quiet, Toad," said the girl. "My aunt does the washing for all the prisoners here. She takes the washing on a Monday, and brings it in on Friday evening. This is a Thursday. Now, you're rich and she's poor. A few pounds would mean a lot to her. I think we could arrange it so that she would let you have her clothes, and you could escape as the washerwoman."

So, next evening, the girl took her aunt into Toad's cell and, in return for his cash, Toad received a cotton print gown, an apron, a shawl, and a black bonnet. He took off his own clothes, put on the washerwoman's and, with a quaking heart, left the cell.

It seemed hours before the great door clicked behind him, but at last he felt fresh air on his brow, and knew that he was free!

He made his way to the railway station but, at the ticket-office, he realised that he had left his coat and waistcoat in his cell, with his keys, matches, watch — and money.

The clerk would not give him a ticket, and Toad wandered down the platform, tears trickling down each side of his nose.

"Hello, Mother!" said the engine driver. "What's the trouble?"

"Oh, sir!" said Toad. "I am a poor washerwoman, and I've lost all my money, and can't pay for a ticket, and I *must* get home somehow!"

"I'll tell you what I'll do," said the good engine driver. "If you'll wash a few shirts for me, I'll give you a ride on my engine."

The Toad scrambled up into the cab of the engine, the guard waved his flag, and the train moved out of the station.

As the speed increased Toad began to think how every minute was bringing him nearer Toad Hall, and friends, and a soft bed to sleep in, and good things to eat, and he began to skip up and down and shout and sing, to the astonishment of the engine driver, who had met washerwomen before, but never one like this. . . .

They had covered many miles when the engine driver looked back. "We're the last train running tonight," he said, "but I can see another. It looks as if we're being pursued."

He looked back again. "They're gaining on us fast!" he said. "The engine is crowded with the queerest lot of people! Policemen waving truncheons, detectives waving revolvers — and they're all shouting the same thing — 'Stop, stop, stop!'"

Toad fell on his knees and pleaded with the engine driver. "Save me," he said. "I am not the washerwoman I seem to be! I am a toad, and I have just escaped from gaol. I only borrowed a motor car — I didn't mean to steal it, really."

"I won't desert you," said the engine driver. "Cheer up, I'll do my best!"

They threw more coal into the engine, and the train sped along, but still the other train slowly gained on them. "There's one thing left," said the driver. "Up ahead is a long tunnel. When we are through I'll brake as hard as I can, and you must jump off and hide in the wood there. Then I'll go full speed ahead again, before they realise you've gone."

The train slowed and Toad jumped, then he rolled down an embankment and ran into the wood and hid until both trains had disappeared.

He walked on through the strange wood until, cold, hungry and tired, he found shelter in a hollow tree and slept till the morning.

Wayfarers All

The Water Rat was restless, and he did not know why. Summer was coming to an end. In the corn fields the field mice and harvest mice were preparing to move house before the harvesters came, and the swallows were making plans for their journey south.

Water Rat lay by the road, and was thinking of the

places that it led to, when a very dusty Rat came into view. The Rat sat beside him, but did not speak.

The wayfarer was lean, and wore small gold earrings. He wore a faded blue jersey, patched blue trousers, and his belongings were tied up in a blue handkerchief.

When he had rested the stranger spoke. "I see by your build that you're a freshwater mariner," he said. "I'm a seafaring rat myself, from the fair city of Constantinople."

Water Rat was intrigued, and asked the stranger to tell him of his voyages.

"On my last voyage," the Sea Rat began, "I went on board a small trading vessel bound for the Grecian Islands. Then we coasted up the Adriatic, to

Venice, a fine city where a rat can wander at his ease! Then we sailed south again, to Sardinia and Corsica, and to Spain, Portugal, France, and on to Cornwall and Devon, and their pleasant harbours."

Spellbound and quivering with excitement, the Water Rat followed the adventurer through stormy bays, into lively harbour bars and up winding coastal rivers. He searched islands for treasure, fished in lagoons and dozed all day on warm white sand.

The Sea Rat still held Water Rat's attention as he stood up. "Now I'll take to the road again," he said. "Come too, young brother. Take the adventure, heed the call, then some day come back and sit by your quiet river with a store of good memories to keep you company." And with that the Sea Rat was gone.

Water Rat returned home in a kind of daze and packed a few things together. After taking a stout stick he was about to leave when Mole appeared at the door. "Where are you off to, Ratty?" asked the Mole.

"Going south, with the rest of them," replied the Water Rat. "To the sea, then onto a ship, and to the shores that are calling me!"

The Mole was alarmed by the far-away look in his friend's eyes. He dragged him inside, threw him down, and held him.

The Rat struggled for a few moments, then lay still, with closed eyes, trembling. Gradually the Rat dozed, then slept deeply.

Mole left him for a time, and returned to find Rat silent and sad. Rat tried to explain what had happened, but now the spell was broken, the magic gone, and he found it hard to understand himself.

Mole turned the talk to the coming harvest. He spoke of the bare fields dotted with sheaves, of reddening apples, browning nuts, jams and preserves to be made ready for the winter, until the Rat began to join in. His eyes brightened, and gradually he became his own cheerful self again.

The Further Adventures of Toad

Toad woke early. He brushed the dry leaves out of his hair, and walked out of the wood onto a road, which was soon joined by a canal. Round a bend came a gaily-painted barge pulled by a horse, its sole occupant a big woman in a sun-bonnet. "Nice morning, ma'am!" she said to Toad.

"I dare say it is, ma'am," said Toad, "to them that's not in sore trouble, like what I am. My married daughter asks me to come to her at once, so off I comes. Now I've lost all my money, and lost my way. My daughter lives near Toad Hall, wherever that is."

"Toad Hall?" replied the barge woman. "I'm going that way myself. I'll give you a lift."

Toad jumped aboard.

"So you're in the washing business?" said the

barge woman as they glided along. "Are you very fond of washing?"

"I love it," said Toad. "Never so happy as when I've got both arms in the wash-tub. But then it comes so easy to me! A real pleasure!"

"What a bit of luck," said the woman. "There's a heap of things in the cabin. If you'll wash them as we go along it'll be a real help to me. I'll know you're enjoying yourself, instead of sitting here idle, looking at the scenery."

Toad was cornered. He fetched tub and soap and set to. A long half hour passed, and Toad got crosser and crosser. Nothing he did altered the state of the washing. His back ached, and his paws were getting all crinkly. He muttered under his breath, and lost the soap for the fiftieth time.

A burst of laughter made Toad look round. "I've been watching you," said the woman. "Washerwoman indeed! You've never washed so much as a dish cloth!"

Toad lost his temper. "You common, *fat* woman!" he shouted. "Don't you dare talk to your betters like that! I am a Toad, a very well-known, respected Toad."

The woman peered under his bonnet. "Well I never! A horrid, nasty, crawly Toad! And in my nice clean barge! I won't have that!"

She grabbed Toad, and he found himself flying through the air, the wind whistling in his ears.

He landed in the canal and rose to the surface

spluttering and wiping the duckweed out of his eyes. He vowed, as he coughed and choked, to be even with the barge woman.

On dry land again, Toad started to run after the barge, wild with indignation. He overtook the barge, then the horse, and unfastened its tow-rope. Then he leapt onto the horse's back, urged it to a gallop, and left the barge far behind.

Toad and the horse had travelled some miles when they came to a gipsy caravan. "Want to sell that there horse of yours?" said the gipsy, who was sitting smoking on an upturned bucket. "A shilling a leg."

Toad considered the offer. "I'll take six shillings and sixpence," he said. "And as much of that delicious stew as I can eat."

The gipsy grumbled, but in the end he counted out six shillings and sixpence into Toad's paw, and gave him a plate of the hot, rich stew.

When Toad could eat no more he set off on his travels again, very pleased with himself, and the way he had outwitted his enemies.

"Ho, ho!" he said. "I am the Toad, the handsome, the popular, the successful Toad!" He made up a song in praise of himself, and sang it at the top of his voice:

"The world has held great heroes,
As history books have showed,
But never a name to go down to fame
Compared with that of Toad!"

There was much more of the same, but too conceited to be written down.

But Toad's pride was shortly to have a severe fall.

After some miles of country lanes he reached the road where he saw approaching — a car. He stepped into the road to ask for a lift, but as the car slowed down Toad turned pale, and his knees shook. The car was the one he had stolen from the Red Lion!

Toad sank down in a miserable heap. "It's all over now!" he said. "Prison again! Dry bread and water again!"

The car stopped, and two gentlemen got out and

looked at Toad. "This is very sad," said one. "A poor washerwoman has fainted."

They lifted Toad into the car, and he realised that they had not recognised him.

"How do you feel now, ma'am?" said one of the gentlemen.

"A great deal better!" said Toad. "Could I sit on the front seat, beside the driver? For the fresh air?"

Soon Toad was seated beside the driver, almost beside himself with pleasure.

After a few minutes he could not resist speaking to the driver. "Please, sir," he said, "could I try and drive the car?"

The driver agreed, and Toad took the wheel. He drove carefully at first, then a little faster, then faster still . . . and faster.

The gentlemen called out, "Be careful, washerwoman!" But this annoyed him, and he went faster still.

"Washerwoman indeed!" shouted Toad. "I am the Toad, the car snatcher, the Toad who always escapes!"

The gentlemen gave a cry of horror. "Seize him!" they shouted.

Toad turned the wheel, the car crashed through a hedge — and landed in a pond! Toad flew through the air and landed with a thump in a meadow. He could see the car in the pond, nearly submerged, and the gentlemen floundering in the water.

Toad set off running as fast as he could, scrambling through hedges, jumping ditches, pounding across fields, till he was breathless, and had to stop to rest.

Just when he was congratulating himself on his escape, a noise behind him made him look round. The driver and two policemen were chasing him!

Toad ran off again, but the pursuers were gaining on him. Suddenly the earth beneath him disappeared and — *splash!* — he found himself in the deep waters of the river!

He tried to grasp the reeds, but the stream was so strong that it tore them from his hands. "Oh my!" he gasped. "If ever I steal a car again!" Then down he went, and came up breathless and spluttering.

He came to a big dark hole in the bank and caught hold of the edge and held on, puffing and panting.

As he stared into the dark hole some bright small thing shone and twinkled in its depths, moving towards him. A face grew gradually around it, and it was a familiar face!

Brown and small, with whiskers.

It was the Water Rat!

Like Summer Tempests Came His Tears

The Rat gripped Toad firmly by the scruff of the neck and gave a great pull until he stood safe and sound, streaked with mud and weed, and with water streaming off him, but happy to have found a friend.

"Oh, Ratty!" he cried. "I've been through such times since I last saw you! Such sufferings! Been in prison — got out, of course! Been thrown into a canal — swam ashore! Stole a horse — sold him! Humbugged everybody — made 'em all do exactly what I wanted! Oh, I *am* a smart Toad!"

"Toad," said the Water Rat firmly, "go upstairs at once and take off that old cotton rag. You look like a washerwoman!"

When Toad had had a wash and changed his clothes, he told Rat of his adventures, dwelling mainly on his own cleverness. The more he talked and boasted, the more silent the Rat became.

"Don't you see what an ass you've been?" said the Rat. "You've been handcuffed, imprisoned, starved, chased, insulted, jeered at — and flung into the canal. And all because you stole a motor car. When are you going to be sensible?"

Toad seemed quite humble suddenly. "Quite right, Ratty!" he said. "I'm going to be a good Toad from now on. We'll have coffee, then I'll stroll down to Toad Hall and set things going again on the old lines!"

"What are you talking about?" cried the Rat. "Haven't you heard about the stoats and weasels?"

"The Wild Wooders?" cried Toad, trembling. "What have they been doing?"

"They've taken Toad Hall."

Toad leaned his elbows on the table and a large tear welled up in each eye and splashed onto the table, *plop! plop!*

The Rat continued. "When you got into trouble," he said, "it was talked of even in the Wild Wood. Animals took sides. The river-bankers stuck up for you, but the Wild Wood animals said you were done for this time! One dark night a band of weasels, armed to the teeth, crept up to the front entrance of Toad Hall. Ferrets took over the offices, stoats occupied the conservatory and billiard-room, and opened the French windows leading on to the lawn.

"The Mole and the Badger (who were living at Toad Hall to keep it aired) were sitting by the fire when the villains burst in, but what could they do against hundreds? They were beaten with sticks, and thrown out, and the Wild Wooders have been living in Toad Hall ever since. Lying in bed half the day. Eating your grub and drinking your drink, and telling everybody that they've come to stay."

"I'll jolly soon see about that!" said Toad, and off he went to Toad Hall.

A ferret with a gun stood by the gate. "Who's there?" said the ferret.

"Stuff and nonsense!" said Toad angrily. "What do you mean, talking to me like that? I'll —"

The ferret didn't speak, but — bang! — a bullet whistled over Toad's head.

Toad scampered off and told the Water Rat what had happened.

"What did I tell you?" said the Rat. "You must just wait."

But Toad didn't want to give up, and rowed in Rat's boat up the creek that led to the boat house. He was just passing under the bridge when — crash! — a great stone, dropped from above, smashed through the bottom of the boat. It filled and sank, and Toad found himself in deep water. Looking up, he saw two stoats leaning over the bridge. "It will be your head next, Toady!" they called.

Toad returned to Rat's house and told him what had happened.

"What did I tell you?" said the Rat. "We can do nothing until we see the Mole and the Badger. They have been camping out in the open, watching over your house and planning how to get it back for you."

Not long after, the Mole and the Badger arrived at the Rat's house.

"The stoats are on guard everywhere," said the Badger. "It's useless to think of attacking the place. But there is another way in. An underground passage that leads from the river bank into the middle of Toad Hall. A very secret passage."

The Badger outlined his plan. "There's going to be a banquet tomorrow night, and all the weasels will be in the dining hall, eating and drinking. No guns, no sticks, no swords! And the tunnel leads up to the pantry, next to the dining hall."

"We'll creep into the pantry —" cried the Mole.

"— with our pistols and swords and sticks —" shouted the Rat.

"— and rush in—," said the Badger.

"— and whack 'em, and whack 'em, and whack 'em!" cried the Toad, running round and round the room, jumping over the chairs.

"Very well then," said the Badger. "Our plan is settled."

It was late, so with that they all went off to bed.

The Return of Ulysses

Next day, when it began to grow dark, they got ready for the expedition. Each animal wore a belt with a sword and cutlass. They also had a pair of pistols, a policeman's truncheon, several sets of handcuffs, some bandages and plasters, and a flask and a sandwich case.

Badger took a lantern in one paw, grasped a large stick in the other and said, "Now then, follow me!"

He led them along by the river, then suddenly swung himself over the edge into a hole in the river bank a little above the water. They were in the secret passage, and the expedition had begun!

It was cold and dark and damp and low, and they groped and shuffled along with their ears pricked and their paws on their pistols until Badger said, "We ought to be under the Hall by now."

Suddenly they heard, apparently over their heads, a murmur of sound, as though people were shouting and cheering and stamping on the floor and hammering on tables.

The passage began to slope upwards, and they hurried on until the passage came to a full stop. They were standing under the trap door that led up into the pantry.

There was such a noise that there was little danger of their being overheard, and the four of them heaved the trap door back, and hoisted themselves into the pantry, with only a door between them and their enemies.

The Badger took a firm grip of his stick with both paws, glanced at his comrades and cried: "The hour is come! Follow me!"

He flung the door open wide.

My! What a squealing and a squeaking and a screeching filled the air!

The terrified weasels dived under the tables, and the ferrets rushed madly to the fireplace and got jammed in the chimney. Tables and chairs were upset, and glass and china crashed to the floor as the four Heroes strode into the room!

The mighty Badger, his whiskers bristling, his great stick whistling through the air. Mole, black and grim, shouting an awful war cry. Rat, desperate and determined, his belt bulging with weapons. Toad, swollen to twice his normal size, leaping into the air.

There were only four of them, but to the panic-stricken weasels the room seemed to be full of monstrous animals, and they fled with squeals of terror this way and that, through the windows, up the chimney, anywhere to get out of the way of those terrible sticks.

It was soon over; in five minutes the room was cleared. All that could be heard through the broken windows were the shrieks of terrified weasels escaping across the lawn.

Badger told the others to set a table on its legs again, pick up knives, forks, plates and glasses, and see what they could find to eat. "Look lively, Toad!" he said. "We've got your house back for you, and you don't even offer us a sandwich."

They found a cold chicken, some trifle, and quite a lot of lobster salad, and in the pantry they found a basketful of French rolls, and cheese, butter and celery.

They ate their supper in great contentment, and soon after crawled into bed, safe in Toad's ancestral home, won back by great valour — and properly handled sticks.

The following morning Badger spoke to Toad. "We really ought to have a banquet, you know, to celebrate," he said. "It's expected of you — in fact, it's the rule."

"Alright," said Toad. "Anything to oblige."

"The invitations will have to be written," Badger went on, "and you've got to write 'em. Now sit down at the table, and if you stick at it we'll have them sent out by lunch."

"What!" cried the Toad. "Stop indoors and write a lot of rotten letters, when I want to go round my property, and swagger about and enjoy myself! Certainly not! I'll — stop a minute, though! Er, why, of course, dear Badger. You wish it done, and it shall be done."

Badger wondered what had made Toad change his mind so suddenly, but he decided to say nothing, and left the room.

Toad hurried to the writing-table. A fine idea had occurred to him. He *would* write the invitations, and he would take care to mention the leading part he had taken in the fight. He would hint at his adventures and his triumphs, and would give a programme of entertainment for the evening — something like this:

SPEECH.. BY TOAD
(There will be other speeches by
Toad during the evening)

ADDRESS .... BY TOAD
SYNOPSIS — Our Prison System — The
Waterways of England — Horse Dealing —
Property — Back to the Land — A
Typical English Squire

SONG.. BY TOAD
(composed by himself)

OTHER COMPOSITIONS .... BY TOAD

The idea pleased him mightily, and he worked
very hard to finish all the letters before giving them
to a rather bedraggled weasel to deliver for him.

At lunch Toad was so uppish and inflated that the

Mole began to suspect something, and the Rat and the Badger exchanged significant glances.

After lunch they tackled him. "Now, look here, Toad," said the Rat. "It's about this banquet. There will be no speeches and no songs. Your songs are all boasting and vanity, and your speeches all self praise and —"

"Gas," put in the Badger.

"It's for your own good, Toady," went on the Rat. "You know you *must* turn over a new leaf sooner or later, and now seems a splendid time to begin."

Toad thought long and hard. At last he raised his head. "You have conquered, my friends," he said. "I will be a very different Toad from now on. You shall never have to blush for me again. But, oh dear, this is a hard world!"

And, pressing a handkerchief to his face, he left the room with faltering footsteps.

"Badger," said the Rat, "I feel like a brute."

"I know," said the Badger gloomily. "But it had to be done. This good fellow has got to live here, and be respected. Would you have him mocked and jeered at by stoats and weasels?"

"Of course not," said the Rat. "And, talking of weasels, it's lucky we came upon that little weasel with Toad's invitations. I looked at one or two; they were disgraceful. Mole is writing new ones now."

At last the hour of the banquet began to draw near and Toad sat in his bedroom, melancholy and thoughtful. Then gradually he began to smile long, slow smiles. Then he took to giggling.

At last he got up, locked the door, drew the curtains, collected all the chairs and arranged them in a semi-circle, and took up his position in front of them, swelling visibly. Then be bowed, coughed twice, and sang to his imaginary audience.

TOAD'S LAST LITTLE SONG!

The Toad — came — home!
There was panic in the parlour and howling in the hall,
There was crying in the cow shed and shrieking in the stall,
When the Toad — came — home!

When the Toad — came — home!
There was smashing in of window and crashing in of door,
There was chivvying of weasels that fainted on the floor,
When the Toad — came — home!

Bang! go the drums!
The trumpeters are tooting and the soldiers are saluting,
And the cannon they are shooting and the motor cars are hooting,
As the — Hero — comes!

Shout — Hooray!
And let each one of the crowd try and shout it very loud,
In honour of the animal of whom you're justly proud,
For it's Toad's — great — day!

He sang this very loud, and when he had done, he sang it all over again.

Then he heaved a deep sigh; a long, long, long sigh, and went quietly down the stairs to greet his guests.

All the animals cheered when he entered, and crowded round to congratulate him and say nice things about his courage, and his cleverness, and his fighting qualities. But Toad only smiled faintly and murmured, "Not at all!" or sometimes, for a change, "On the contrary!"

Otter came forward with a shout, threw his arm round Toad's neck, and tried to take him round the room in triumphal progress, but Toad remarked gently, as he disengaged himself, "Badger was the mastermind; the Mole and the Water Rat bore the brunt of the fighting. I merely served in the ranks, and did little or nothing."

The Badger had ordered the best of everything, and the banquet was a great success. There was much talking and laughter among the animals, but through it all Toad looked down his nose and murmured pleasant nothings to the animals on either side of him. At intervals he stole a glance at the Badger and the Rat, and always when he looked they were staring at each other with their mouths open, and this gave him the greatest satisfaction.

As the evening wore on there were some knockings on the table and cries of, "Toad! Speech! Speech from Toad! Song! Mr Toad's song!" But Toad shook his head gently, raised one paw in mild protest and, by pressing delicacies on his guests, and by topical small talk, made it obvious that the banquet was being run on strictly conventional lines.

He was indeed an altered Toad!

After this climax, the four animals continued to lead their lives in great joy and contentment, undisturbed by further risings or invasions. After consulting his friends, Toad selected a handsome gold chain and locket set with pearls, which he sent to the gaoler's daughter with a letter that even Badger thought modest and grateful. The engine driver was properly thanked and compensated for his trouble and, under severe compulsion from Badger, even the barge woman was paid the value of her horse.

Sometimes, in the course of long summer evenings, the friends would take a stroll together in the Wild Wood, now successfully tamed as far as they were concerned. It was pleasing to see how respectfully they were greeted by the inhabitants, and how the mother weasels would bring their young ones to the mouths of their holes and say, pointing, "Look, baby! There goes the great Mr Toad! And that's the gallant Water Rat, a terrible fighter! And yonder comes the famous Mr Mole, of whom you have often heard your father tell!"

But when the infants were quite beyond control, they would quieten them by telling how, if they didn't hush, the terrible Badger would come to get them. This was unfair to Badger, who was rather fond of children, but it never failed to have its full effect.